Copyright © 1996 by Nord-Süd Verlag AG, Gossau Zürich, Switzerland.
First published in Switzerland under the title *Das Blaue Monster*.
English translation copyright © 1996 by North-South Books Inc.

First published in the United States, Great Britain, Canada,
Australia, and New Zealand in 1996 by North-South Books,
an imprint of Nord-Süd Verlag AG, Gossau Zürich, Switzerland.

Distributed in the United States by North-South Books Inc., New York.

Library of Congress Cataloging-in-Publication Data is available.
A CIP catalogue record for this book is available from The British Library.
ISBN 1-55858-556-7 (trade binding)
1 3 5 7 9 TB 10 8 6 4 2
ISBN 1-55858-557-5 (library binding)
1 3 5 7 9 LB 10 8 6 4 2
Printed in Belgium

*For information about our books, and the authors
and artists who create them, visit our web site at:*
http://www.northsouth.com

The Blue Monster

By Ingrid Ostheeren · Illustrated by Christa Unzner

Translated by Rosemary Lanning

NORTH-SOUTH BOOKS · NEW YORK · LONDON

In a few days it would be Anna's birthday.

"All I want is a dog," she told her parents. "Nothing else."

Her father laughed at that, but her mother groaned. "Heavens, no!" she said.

"If I can't have a dog, I'll wish for a monster instead!" Anna shouted at them.

Her parents thought this was very funny. Grown-ups don't believe in monsters, you see. Anna believed in monsters. And she wasn't afraid of them. Maybe some monsters were huge and dangerous, but there were nice ones, too. Anna was sure of that. And she truly believed that one night there would be a monster under her bed. It would be a nice monster, but just in case, she always jumped into bed from the other side of the room, so the monster wouldn't be able to grab her ankles if it turned out to be not so nice after all.

In the middle of the night Anna suddenly woke up. The moon was shining brightly through her window, and there was a strange noise coming from under her bed. It was something between a sigh and a sneeze and a snort. Only a monster could make a noise like that! Anna lay very still. Then she heard the noise again.

"Are you hiding under my bed, Monster?" Anna asked bravely.

"No, I'm not," a deep voice replied.

"Don't tell lies, Monster. You are under there!" said Anna.

"No, I'm not."

"Then why is your voice coming from down there?" Anna asked.

"Don't know," muttered the monster.

"Come out!" Anna demanded.

"All right," said the monster. "You won't be frightened of me, will you?"

"No, I won't," said Anna. "As long as you don't do anything nasty to me."

"Of course I won't," promised the monster. And then it came out.

The monster was blue and enormous. As it eased itself out from under the bed, it grew even bigger and rounder. It stared at Anna and Anna stared back. And then the monster smiled, and Anna smiled too. It was a nice monster. She could tell.

"I'm hungry," said the monster. "I've come a long way. You wanted me here. Now you'd better feed me."

Anna squeezed past the monster. She tiptoed downstairs, went into the kitchen, and got a jar of peanut butter.

"That looks good," said the monster. Then it opened its mouth, popped in the peanut butter, and gulped it down. "Very tasty," it said. "Though I prefer a sweeter filling."

"Where is the peanut butter?" asked Anna's mother at breakfast.

Anna wondered whether she should tell a lie, but decided not to. "The monster ate it, jar and all," she said.

"Really, Anna!" her mother reproached her. "How can you talk such nonsense? There's no such thing as monsters, and you know it!"

There was nothing more Anna could say.

That afternoon, when her parents were out, Anna took the monster into the living room.

"It's nice here!" said the monster, sitting down in an armchair. The chair creaked, then it groaned, then it gave a loud crack!

"Naughty monster!" scolded Anna. "You've broken the chair. You're much too heavy to sit on the furniture."

The monster frowned. "Me, too heavy?" it said. Then it smiled. "I can make myself as light as a feather if I want to," it boasted.

"I wish you'd thought of that before," said Anna.

Anna's parents looked serious and shook their heads when Anna explained how the monster had broken the chair.

"It is a very heavy monster," said Anna. "And it had forgotten to make itself as light as a feather before it sat down."

"We really ought to give her a dog for her birthday," said her father when Anna had gone to bed. "She's making up these monster stories because she's so disappointed."

"I'm going to Bernie's party this afternoon," Anna told the monster the next morning. "But you can't come. You would scare my friends. You're so big and so . . . blue!"

That hurt the monster's feelings. "I'm quite good-looking for a monster," it said grumpily. Then it explained how it would be invisible to everyone except Anna anyway. So Anna decided to let it come to the party, as long as it promised not to break anything.

The monster promised.

At the party the monster sat in the corner, good as gold, watching the children playing by the swimming pool. It really did seem to be invisible, so Anna relaxed and joined in the games. After a while she forgot the monster was there at all. That was a mistake. Because when she went back to the pool, she got a nasty shock. There stood the monster, right at the end of the diving board, holding its nose.

"Don't jump!" she shouted. But it was too late! The monster jumped.

The monster hit the water with a wallop, splashing it in all directions. When it climbed out and strolled away, there were only a few puddles left at the bottom of the pool.

"Amazing!" said Bernie. "That must have been a tidal wave. I've read all about them!"

The other children nodded thoughtfully. Anna said nothing. She glared at the monster, who lay on the grass and grinned.

The next morning Anna's mother started to make her birthday cake. The monster squeezed itself into a corner to keep out of Mother's way. Anna had promised to give it a piece of cake, and it was looking forward to that.

When Anna's mother went out to answer the phone, the monster came and peered into the mixing bowl.

"Is that cake?" it asked, and before Anna could say anything it scooped up the cake mixture and gulped it all down.

"Cake tastes yummy!" it said, smacking its lips.

When Anna's mother came back, the monster quickly hid behind the door.

"Where on earth is the cake mixture?" asked Mother.

"The monster gobbled it up," said Anna. "It's standing over there, looking ashamed. Do you see, it's turned purple with embarrassment. It's blue, normally."

"I won't stand for any more of this nonsense," Mother said crossly, and sent Anna to her room.

That night her parents sat and talked about Anna and the monster. "The business with the cake was the last straw," said her mother. "What are we going to do with the child?"

"She's only making up these silly stories about the monster because she so wants a puppy," said her father. "Let's buy her a puppy tomorrow. Then we'll hear no more about the monster."

"I hope you're right," said Anna's mother.

Anna lay in bed, cuddling her teddy. "Tomorrow's my birthday," she told the monster. "Are you happy for me? I want a dog. Maybe if I'm lucky I'll get one."

The monster was silent for a while. Then it said, "You will get one. But tomorrow I will be gone. I won't be able to go to your birthday party. I only come before birthdays, and stay until I'm sure children's wishes are going to come true."

"Dear Monster," said Anna. "Please don't go. I would miss you!"

The monster scratched its nose thoughtfully.

"We'll see," it said.

"You know," said Anna, "we could have fun together, you and I and the puppy. What shall we call him? He must have a name. And you too, Monster. Monster?"

The monster had vanished!

Anna ran to the window, but there was no sign of him there, only a full, golden moon.

She turned sadly to get into bed. Then she saw it. Lying on the quilt was a monster! It was small and soft, no bigger than her teddy—maybe even a bit smaller. And it was as light as a feather. Anna took it in her arms and gave it a monster hug.